THE BIG BLUEBERRY BARF-OFF!

ROTTEN SCHOOL

GROWTH • LEARNING • PIZZA!

THE BIG BLUEBERRY BARF-OFF!

R.L. STINE

Illustrations by Trip Park

SCHOLASTIC INC.

New York Toronto London Auckland Sydney
Mexico City New Delhi Hong Kong Buenos Aires

ISBN-13: 978-0-439-82229-9
ISBN-10: 0-439-82229-7

12 11 10 9 8 7 6 5 4 3 2 1   6 7 8 9 10 11/0

Printed in the U.S.A.   40

First Scholastic paperback printing, November 2006

Cover and interior design by mjcdesign

To Phil Silvers
–RLS

For Laura,
you gave me my
four biggest fans.
–TP

CONTENTS

Morning
Announcements 1

1. Breakfast in Bed 4

2. Feenman and Crench 11

3. A Crowd Gathers 16

4. My Archenemy 20

5. My Million-Dollar Watch . . . 29

6. Headmaster Upchuck 36

7. Chipmunk 42

8. My Friend Beast 48

9. Pie fight 54

10. Allergic to Pie 61

11. 25 Chocolate Cakes 66

12. Jennifer Ecch 69

13. The Horrible Accident 73

14. 25 Blueberry Pies 79

15. Eat Pie! 84

16. The Big Barf-Off 89

17. Busted 98

18. Dance Lessons 104

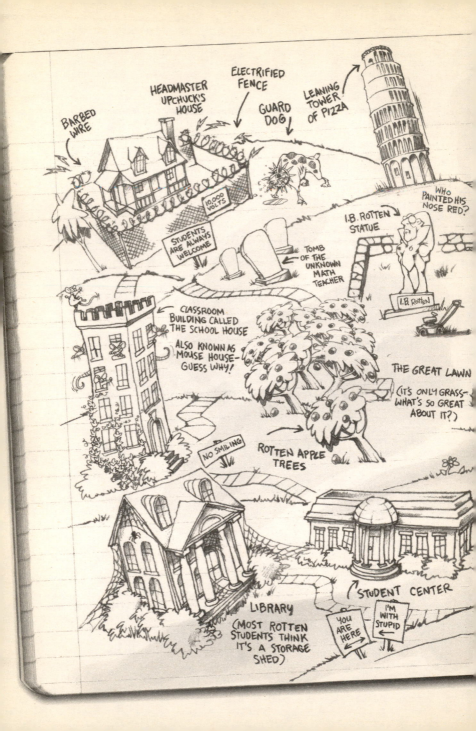

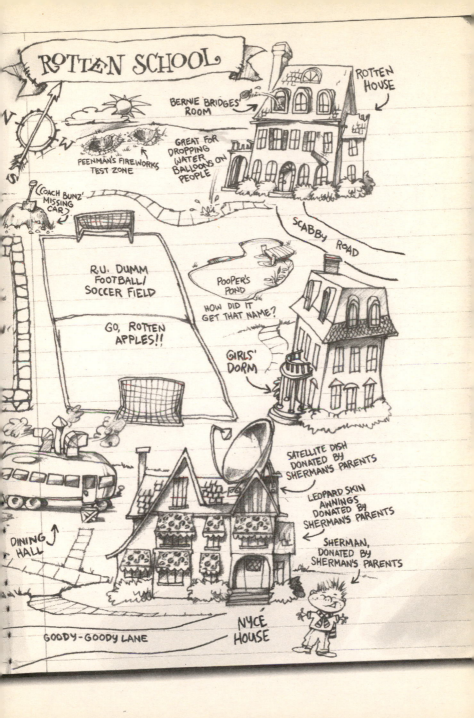

MORNING ANNOUNCEMENTS

Good morning, everyone. This is Headmaster Upchuck. I hope all of our Rotten students are ready to start the day.

I will be giving important announcements over the loudspeaker every morning. I hope we can get this fixed so it doesn't squeal and whistle. Ow! That really hurt my ears!

Doesn't anybody know how to stop that?

I guess not. OWW!

Anyway, here are today's important Morning Announcements....

A special reminder from Coach Bunz to our Third-Grade Swim Team. Please remember that the No Peeing in the Pool rule is still being enforced.

Congratulations to the Volunteer Club of Nyce House. They have collected over fifty pounds of old newspaper. They are asking if anyone has any idea what to do with it.

Mr. Farrhowt has asked me to make this special announcement to students in his Class for Beginning Rappers...."Yo. What up, dawgs? We be breaking it down. Bring the bling. Bust a move, yo."

The stomach pump is missing again from Nurse Hanley's office. Please return it and no questions will be asked.

I want to congratulate fifth grader Eric Spindlebag. Eric won the I CARE DEEPLY ABOUT MY SCHOOL essay contest. His winning essay was titled "Whatever."

Members of the after-school Dental Hygiene Club announce that third grader Billy Sligg will be showing off his new retainer at dinner tonight.

A reminder that tonight is Island Night in the Dining Hall. Chef Baloney will be serving a special menu with a tropical theme. I'm sure you will all enjoy the chef's Coconut-Crusted Fist of Buffalo… Plankton Surprise…Trout Lips in a Sponge Sauce… and Lizard Pudding. Enjoy!

Chapter 1

BREAKFAST IN BED

Tweet tweet tweet.

My bird alarm clock woke me up gently. I opened my big brown eyes and smiled. Catch those dimples in my cheeks. I always wake up with a smile.

Hey, I'm Bernie Bridges. Why shouldn't I smile?

I had no idea today was the day it would all start. No idea what I'd find when I stepped outside.

No idea that today would lead to the Biggest Pie Battle in the history of the school—maybe the WORLD!

How could I know? I was still half-asleep.

I raised my head. I could hear the other guys in my dorm rushing out to the Dining Hall to get breakfast.

Hey, am I going to hurry? No way. I settled back on my feather pillow and smiled some more.

I knew my faithful friend Belzer would bring my breakfast on a tray. Belzer brings me breakfast in bed every morning.

Good kid, Belzer.

I sat up and stretched. "Bernie, you've got it made!" I told myself. I talk to myself a lot. I mean, who *else* understands pure genius?

I put on my glasses. Sunlight poured through my window. The curtains fluttered in a cool breeze. I gazed at my favorite poster on the wall, the big poster of ME.

You probably go home every day after school. Poor sucker. My parents travel all the time. So they sent me to the Rotten School, my home away from home.

It's a boarding school, see. That means I get to live in a dorm with my friends. No parents.

How cool is that?

Actually, we live in an old house called Rotten House. A whole bunch of my fourth- and fifth-grade friends live on my floor. We claimed the third floor because it's good for dropping water balloons out the window.

Mrs. Heinie doesn't know about that. But she knows just about everything else that goes on here.

Mrs. Heinie is our dorm mother. She's really nice, but she has a job to do. That means she's always snooping around, sniffing in corners, keeping an eye on us.

Mrs. Heinie is also our fourth-grade core teacher. She has her own apartment in the attic.

"Yo, dude," I called out to Belzer as he carried in my breakfast tray.

"Morning, Big B," he said. He's a chubby guy with red hair that falls down over his eyes, and he has freckles everywhere. He set my breakfast tray down and pulled off the cover.

"Good work!" I said, slapping him on the back.

"Hey, thanks, Bernie." He smiled that lopsided smile of his. Anyone can see his braces haven't helped at all.

Maybe I'll adjust them for him later. I'm a *wizard* with a pair of pliers.

"You're looking sharp today, Belzer," I said.

Belzer was wearing his Rotten School blazer and tie. But under the tie, he wore a white T-shirt with bright red letters that said: ASK ME ABOUT MY ALLERGIES.

I once made the mistake of asking Belzer about his allergies. He said, "I don't have any. I just like the shirt."

I started to eat my breakfast.

"I strained the pulp from your orange juice," Belzer said.

"Good work, dude."

"And I got you extra blueberries for your pancakes."

"Excellent, Belzer. The soft blueberries, right? Not the chewy ones."

"Yeah. I tested each one," Belzer said. "And your toast is just the way you like it."

I picked up a slice of toast and checked it out. "Light on one side, dark on the other. Perfect, Belzer. Good work, fella!"

"Thank you, Big B." He flashed his crooked smile.

I started to dig into the pancakes. I looked up. Two guys stood in the doorway. They were eyeing my breakfast hungrily.

"Well, well. Look who's here!" I said.

Chapter 2

FEENMAN AND CRENCH

My two best buddies, Feenman and Crench, came walking in.

Feenman and Crench are tall and lean and goofy-looking. They grin a lot and punch each other a lot and can never stand still.

Feenman has long, stringy hair that hangs down like a mop. Crench's hair is short and flat. That's because his *head* is flat!

"Whussup, Big B?" Crench asked.

Feenman reached for a slice of toast. I had to slap his hand away.

Belzer, Feenman, and Crench are crammed into the tiny room across from me. They *insisted* that I have my own room. They know I need a lot of space for planning and scheming.

"Okay, guys. Give me the report," I said. "How are the Bernie Bridges T-shirts selling?"

Crench shook his head. "They're not selling, Bernie."

"How many have you sold?" I asked. "Twenty? Thirty?"

"None," Feenman replied. "N-u-n-n. None."

"I think you spell none with a y," Crench said.

"Never mind the spelling lesson," I said. "Why aren't kids buying the Bernie Bridges T-shirts?"

"Because they're itchy," Crench said. "Kids don't want to pay five dollars for a T-shirt that makes them scratch all day."

"But it's got my picture on it!" I said.

Crench shook his head again. "Bernie, we told you not to make the T-shirts out of rope. No one wants to wear a rope T-shirt."

"But rope is cheaper than cotton," I said. "I have to make a profit, don't I?"

Feenman shrugged. "We couldn't even sell them to the third graders, Big B. I think you should give up."

"Give up?" I cried. I jumped to my feet. "Give up?

How *dare* you use those words with me! Do I ever give up for *you?*"

They lowered their heads. "No, Bernie," they both answered.

Feenman made another grab for the toast. I jabbed him with my fork.

"I never give up," I said. "I do everything for you guys. I do the impossible for you guys—don't I?"

"Yes, you do, Big B," Belzer said. He turned to Feenman and Crench. "Who convinced the cook that a Milky Way bar is a *vegetable?*"

"Bernie did," they both answered.

"And who convinced Headmaster Upchuck to make Game Boys a required *school supply?*" Belzer asked.

"Bernie did."

"Who convinced Mrs. Heinie to give extra credit for putting your name at the top of your test?" Belzer asked.

"Bernie did!" Feenman and Crench replied.

"Don't forget wedgies," I whispered to Belzer.

"Oh, right!" Belzer said. "Who got Coach Bunz to make Giving Wedgies a varsity sport?"

14

"Bernie did," they answered. "Bernie did!"

"You're the *best*, Big B!" Belzer cried.

We all cheered and slapped high fives and did the secret Rotten House handshake.

"So get out there and sell those rope T-shirts," I said.

"Sell, sell, sell!" Feenman and Crench shouted, pumping their fists in the air. And they hurried out the door.

Chapter 3

A CROWD GATHERS

A few minutes later, I put on my school uniform and headed downstairs. I didn't want to be late for my first class with Mrs. Heinie.

I stopped in the front hall. From the back of the house I could hear screams and a sharp, stinging sound—*slap slap slap*.

Just some guys having fun in the shower room. Slapping one another silly with wet towels.

The Rotten School is a very old school. And we have a lot of wonderful, old traditions here. Wet-towel smacking is one of our favorites.

I stepped back and listened....

SMAAACK.

"Ow!"
"Good one, Zuckerman!"

SMAAACK!

"Ow!"
"Good one, Klooper!"

Hey, I love the sound of snapping towels. Know why? Because I rent out the towels.

Guys don't mind paying fifty cents a towel when they know they're getting a good *smack* for their money.

I stepped out the front door and down the steps. Then I started to jog across the Great Lawn to class.

It was a sunny September day. The grass sparkled. The sky was cloudless and blue.

My backpack bounced on my back. It was empty. Belzer was carrying all of my books for me.

Good kid, Belzer.

I stopped when I saw the crowd of kids on the grass. They were gathered around the statue of I. B. Rotten. What were they doing there?

I. B. Rotten was the guy who started this school a hundred years ago. Guess who he named it after?

Old I. B. was my kind of guy: a zillionaire. He made his money by owning grocery stores all over the U.S., called Rotten Food Shoppes.

The statue of I. B. Rotten stands on a pedestal in the center of the Great Lawn. He has a very long nose that looks like an animal snout. He has tiny, round eyes and short, furry hair.

He looks a lot like an anteater wearing a suit. But *The Rotten School Student Guidebook* says on page three that he was human.

Last spring, someone who I won't name— Feenman—snuck out one night and painted the long nose on the statue bright red.

Feenman is really into painting things red. It's kind of his hobby.

Anyway, they tried for months, but no one could get the paint off the statue. So now it looks like I. B. Rotten always has a very bad cold.

Why were all the kids huddling around the statue this morning? I saw Feenman and Crench in the crowd. I hurried over to them.

"What's up? What's all the excitement?"

Chapter 4

My Archenemy

Crench didn't say a word. He just pointed.

I let out a groan when I saw the kid in the center of the crowd. That spoiled rich kid, Sherman Oaks. My archenemy.

He had a big, toothy grin on his face. He was holding up a glowing object, waving it around to the crowd.

Sherman lives in the dorm across from Rotten House, the dorm we all hate. I can't even say the name of his dorm. When I say it, my teeth curl, my nose twitches, and my lips swell up like salamis.

It's called…It's called…(deep breath, Bernie)… NYCE House.

What kind of kid would want to live in a dorm called *Nyce* House?

More kids joined the crowd around Sherman. Kids were *oohing* and *aahing*.

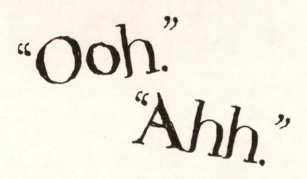

"Ooh." "Ahh."

Something glowed like gold on Sherman's wrist. What was he showing off this time?

I started to push my way through the crowd. But I stopped when I saw April-May June standing next to Sherman. She was holding on to his arm, *smiling* at him.

April-May June. The hottest, coolest girl in the whole fourth grade. April-May has wavy blond hair,

shiny blue eyes, and a smile almost as dazzling as mine. The girl is totally crazy nuts about me. Only she doesn't know it yet.

I elbowed some gawking fifth graders aside and stepped up to Sherman. "What is that on your wrist?" I asked. "Some kind of skin rash? Have you tried calamine lotion?"

Sherman turned and flashed me his smug, sixty-five-tooth smile. "It's my new digital watch, Bernie," he said. He shoved it in front of my face. The sunlight beamed off the gold band, so bright it hurt my eyes.

"It has forty-two different functions," Sherman said. "And it cost five hundred dollars. My parents

sent it to me because they think they can buy my love with fancy electronics."

My mouth dropped open. *Forty-two functions?*

April-May squeezed Sherman's arm. "Show him what it can do, Shermy."

Shermy??

MY *girlfriend* (only she didn't know it yet) was calling Sherman Oaks *Shermy?*

Sherman swung the watch up so everyone could see it.

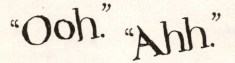

Give me a break. Why didn't they stop all that *oohing* and *ahhing*?

"Well, it's a camera, of course," Sherman said. "And a video player. A phone. A palm pilot. An MP3 player. A printer. A tiny computer. Here's the keyboard."

He pushed a button, and a computer keyboard slid out. Then he pushed another button, and a piano keyboard appeared.

"It has a small George Foreman grill on it,"
Sherman announced. He opened the lid and showed
it to everyone.

"Ooh." "Ahh."

I turned to Crench. "It's *got* to weigh two hundred pounds," I snickered. "He'll sprain his wrist."

"Ooh." "Ahh."

That was Crench oohing and ahhing! Traitor!

Sherman showed how he downloads all his homework onto his watch and e-mails it to Mrs. Heinie. I tugged April-May aside. I had to pry her fingers off Sherman's arm to pull her away.

"What do you want, Bernie?" she asked. She didn't look at me. Her eyes were still on the watch.

Sherman was showing how he makes his own animated films on the watch.

"April-May, I knew he was boring you with that piece of junk," I said. "How annoying. A watch with only forty-two functions. I mean, that's *so* yesterday."

April-May rolled her beautiful blue eyes. "What do you want, Bernie?"

"Well, they're having dance lessons at the Student Center on Saturday and—"

"No way, Bernie," she said.

"I thought maybe you'd like to come with me and—"

"No way, Bernie," she said.

"Maybe we could take the dance lessons together. You and me. I know I could teach you some awesome new moves."

"No way, Bernie," she said.

"Is that a *yes?*" I asked.

"No way, Bernie," she said.

"I'll take that for a definite *maybe*," I said.

April-May stuck her beautiful nose in the air. "I can't go on Saturday," she said. "Sherman is showing me the twelve hidden compartments in his watch."

Twelve hidden compartments? *Ooh.*

Ahh.

April-May hurried back to Sherman's side. Sherman still had his arm raised. He was snapping the gold wristband in everyone's face, showing off the crisp *snap* of real gold.

April-May held on to his arm and smiled into his smug, sneering face.

The watch…the watch had hypnotized her into thinking Sherman was a good guy.

Forty-two functions. Twelve hidden compartments. Solid gold...

I started to shake. My whole body quivered and quaked. My eyes bulged. My tongue flopped out of my mouth.

Feenman and Crench hurried up beside me. "Bernie, what's wrong?" Feenman asked.

"I've GOT to have that WATCH!" I cried. "It's MINE! I can already feel it on my wrist!"

"But, *how*, Bernie?" Feenman asked. "How are you going to get it?"

Chapter 5

My Million-Dollar Watch

I waited till all the kids hurried off to class. As April-May trotted away, I saw her blow a kiss to Sherman.

How sick is that?

My girlfriend-to-be (who doesn't know it yet) blowing a kiss to Sherman Oaks?

That gave me the dry heaves. I covered it up by pretending I was coughing.

Then I turned and backed Sherman up against the statue of I. B. Rotten. "Sherman, my friend, we have to talk," I said.

Sherman let out a cry. I. B. Rotten's knee was poking him in the back.

He held up the watch. "You want to feel it?" he asked. "Go ahead. I'll let you touch it for ten seconds. But don't get your paw prints all over it."

I gazed at the watch. I started to drool. "A five-hundred-dollar watch, huh?" I said.

Sherman grinned. "Yes. My parents paid cash for it. You can do that when you're filthy rich."

I blinked. The sunlight was reflecting off the shiny watch face.

"It's solid gold," Sherman said. "And did I mention it has forty-two functions?"

"Too bad," I said, lowering my eyes.

"Huh?" Sherman squinted at me. "Excuse me?"

"Too bad," I repeated, shaking my head.

Sherman pulled the watch away from me. "Too bad? What do you mean, Bernie?"

"Too bad," I said. I grabbed his shoulder and squeezed it. "A guy like you walking around with a watch like that. It's sad."

Sherman's mouth dropped open. "Are you crazy? What's sad about it?"

"They sell those in the supermarket," I said. "Check this out." I grabbed his watch and twisted it over. Then I pretended to read the back. "I knew it. It says 'Piggly Wiggly Food Stores' on it."

Sherman jerked the watch away. He squinted at the back. "Huh? A supermarket watch? You've got to be kidding."

"I shouldn't do this," I said. "But you know I'm very generous when it comes to my friends...."

Sherman squinted at me. "Give me a break, Bernie. Since *when* am I your friend?"

"I'll tell you what," I said. "I'll trade you *my* watch for yours."

"Huh? You're joking, right? Ha-ha."

"I know it's a bad deal," I said. "My watch is a lot more valuable than yours. Mine is priceless. It belongs in a museum. But what can I say? I'm a sucker. I'm willing to trade."

I grabbed Sherman's watch and tried to slide it off his wrist. I hoped he didn't see how eager I was.

"Whoa. Wait a minute," he said, cupping his other hand over the watch. "What's so valuable about *your* watch?"

Think fast, Bernie!

"It's from ancient Egypt. It has an engraving of the Egyptian sun god, Ra. I shouldn't tell you this, Sherman. But my watch is probably worth a million dollars."

He stared at my watch. "The ancient sun god, Ra? Really? Let me see it, Bernie." He grabbed my wrist and checked out the watch. "Bernie, that's Mickey Mouse," he said. "Dude, you've got a Mickey Mouse watch."

"It's the sun god, Ra, *disguised* as Mickey Mouse!" I told him. "You don't think Ra would show his own face, do you?"

"Bye, Bernie," Sherman said. He picked up his zebra-skin backpack and started away.

"Wait!" I cried. "I can pay you for the watch. Sherman—look." I pulled a fat wad of dollar bills from my pants pocket. It was my life savings. My Eclipse Money.

Last Saturday night, I sold a bunch of second graders tickets to watch the eclipse of Mars. Two dollars each. They got to sit on the grass and stare at the sky. I told them how lucky they were. I told them the Martian eclipse happens only once every three thousand years.

But the kids were very confused.

"Where is it?"

"I don't see anything."

"I can't see Mars. It's too dark!"

"Of *course* it's completely dark up there," I told them. "That's how you know it's an *eclipse*!"

So the kids had a great time rolling around in the grass, staying up all night, partying with their friends.

And good old Bernie B. made a bundle that night. And now I waved the big wad of cash in front of Sherman's nose.

He sniffed it like a dog.

"It's all yours," I said. "Cash money. For your watch."

Suddenly, a shadow fell over me.

I spun around—and saw Headmaster Upchuck standing right behind me. His eyes weren't on me. They were on the thick wad of cash in my hand.

"Bernie Bridges!" the Headmaster cried. "Young man, what are you doing with all that cash?"

Chapter 6

HEADMASTER UPCHUCK

Think fast AGAIN, Bernie.

I made my eyes go all wide and innocent. "Do you mean this money in my hand, sir?" I asked.

"Yes, that money in your hand," Headmaster Upchuck replied.

The Headmaster is short and squat and bald, and he kind of waddles when he walks. He looks a lot like a duck. Some sixth grade kids say he has webbed feet. But you can't believe sixth graders.

I was surprised to see him out on the Great Lawn. The Headmaster has his own little house and office next to the classroom building. And he seldom leaves it.

"That's a very handsome suit you're wearing, sir," I said. "I like the stripes. Makes you look at least a foot taller."

"Bernie, the cash," he said. "What are you doing with all that money?"

I held the wad of bills tightly in my hand. "This is money I've raised, sir, from all the kids," I said. "It's to build a statue of *you*, sir. Right next to I. B. Rotten."

I gave him a quick, two-fingered salute. "You belong here, sir. You've inspired us all so much. We want to put your statue right here."

"That's nice of you, Bernie," the Headmaster said. "But I really think—"

Sherman pointed to the wad of bills in my hand. "That's the money I donated, sir," he said. "I gave Bernie all that money. That's how much you mean to me, sir."

"Whoa. Wait—" I started to choke.

"I appreciate that, Sherman," Headmaster Upchuck said, patting Sherman on the shoulder. "That's very generous of you."

"But— but—" I sputtered.

"I can't accept these donations, boys," Upchuck said. "Bernie, give Sherman back his money."

I stared at the fat wad of bills. My Eclipse Money. My hard-earned cash. My hand started to shake. "But, sir, your statue. It will give us all such joy!" I said.

"Right now, Bernie," Upchuck snapped. "Give Sherman back his money."

I had no choice.

I handed the cash over to Sherman.

Sherman had a big, evil grin on his face. He knew he was a rat.

A rat who had just won big-time.

He stuffed my money into his sealskin wallet. Then he edged close to Headmaster Upchuck. Sherman slid a hundred-dollar bill from his wallet. He pressed it into the Headmaster's hand. "This is for you, sir," he said. "A little gift from the Oaks family."

Upchuck stared at the hundred-dollar bill. "Sherman, are you trying to bribe me *again?*" he asked.

"Yes, sir," Sherman replied.

"Take it back," the Headmaster said, stuffing it into Sherman's shirt pocket. "Aren't you boys late for class?"

"Class? Yes, sir," I said. "But I would gladly miss class to help build that statue of you. Perhaps we should start by having Sherman return that donation to me?"

The Headmaster started to shake. He made a few sharp quacking sounds. "I'm shaking again," he said. "You always do this to me, Bernie. You always give me the—*quaaack*—shakes. Now get to class!"

"Okay, sir," I said. I gave him another two-fingered salute. "Lovely to see you, sir. I *do* love that suit. Those big shoulders make you look very strong. I know you'll grow into them in no time!"

"BERNIE! GET TO CLASS!" he screamed.

"QUACK!
QUAAAACK!"

He started quacking at the top of his lungs and tearing out his hair with both hands. (Only he didn't have any hair.)

"GO AWAY! QUACK! GO AWAY!"

I can take a hint.

I took off, running across the grass to the School House building.

Talk about rotten mornings!

Sherman tricked me out of my money. And he still had the watch.

I needed it. *Needed* it!

I gazed up at the sun, rising golden and bright over the school grounds. It wasn't as bright as that watch.

I had to have it. But how?

How?

That night at dinner, I knew how I would do it. It all came to me in the crunch of a pizza crust....

Chapter 7

CHIPMUNK

That evening, I was climbing the stairs to my room in Rotten House. I stopped to straighten the framed portrait of me that I had hung on the second-floor landing.

I heard a soft sound. Squeaky. Sniffling.

Was someone crying?

I don't like crying. I like my guys to be happy, cheerful.

I poked my head into the first room. Three bunk beds were jammed into this room. In one bottom bunk, a kid sat hunched over, his face buried in his hands. His shoulders heaved up and down. He was definitely crying.

"Chipmunk? What's up?" I asked. I stepped over two weeks of dirty laundry to get to his bed.

My friend Chipmunk raised his head. He had tear stains on his puffy cheeks. His eyes were red and runny.

I guess I don't have to describe Chipmunk to you. You can probably figure out how he got that name.

He was wearing faded jeans, and a gray T-shirt that said SHY PEOPLE RULE! in tiny letters. He wiped his runny nose with the front of his T-shirt.

"Chipmunk, get into your school uniform, dude," I said. "It's almost dinnertime."

"I can't go to dinner," Chipmunk said in his whispery mouse voice. "I can't leave the dorm, Bernie. I have to stay in my room for at least two weeks."

"Excuse me?" I said. "Are you sick?" I jumped back. "You're not contagious—are you?"

Chipmunk lowered his head again. "No. I'm not sick. Look at me. Look at my hair, Bernie. Someone…someone snuck down here last night while I was sleeping—and gave me a haircut." He let out a sob.

I stared at his head. It looked like a patchy quilt with some of the pieces missing. He had sprouts of hair surrounded by big, bald squares.

"At least they left you two ears," I said. "Did you ever meet One-Ear Schmidt? He transferred to another school after his haircut last year."

Chipmunk let out a long, sad sigh. "I just have to stay in my room till it grows out," he said.

"Turn around," I said. "Let's see who did this to you."

Chipmunk turned so I could see the back of his head.

"I knew it!" I cried. "It was one of those creeps from Nyce House! He carved a big N on the back of your head."

"He did?" Chipmunk covered his face with his hands again. "An *N* on the back of my head?"

"Sherman Oaks is behind this," I said. "Do you believe it? Jerks from Nyce House sneaking into our dorm and giving my guys haircuts while they sleep?"

I slapped Chipmunk on the back. "One more reason to pay them back—right? Leave it to Bernie. I'll show these jerks they can't carve letters in our hair!"

Chipmunk shook his head. "I don't care about that," he said. "I'm ruined, Bernie. Ruined."

"No way," I said. "Chipmunk, are you kidding me? Hel-lo. This is an awesome new look for you."

He squinted at me. "Huh?"

"It's totally punk," I said. I picked up a paper clip from the floor. "Here. Put this on one ear. Awesome. The punk look is perfect for you. *Everyone* will be imitating it. You'll see. Guys will *beg* you to tell them how you did it."

Chipmunk's eyes brightened. "You really think so?"

"Of course I do." I slapped him on the back. "Now, get dressed for dinner. People are waiting in the Dining Hall to see your new look."

He jumped to his feet. "Okay, Bernie." He had a smile on his face. But then the smile fell.

"Bernie…what about the *N*?" he asked.

I stopped at the door. "You're from Nebraska, right?" I asked.

"Yeah. Omaha."

"Well, okay!" I said. "No problem, dude. Tell everyone the *N* stands for Nebraska. Then just watch—in a few days, the other guys will *all* be cutting their state initials into their heads. No kidding."

"Thanks, Bernie," Chipmunk said. He had a big grin on his face. "*N* for Nebraska. Thanks a lot!" He flashed me a thumbs-up.

I turned and climbed the stairs to my room. I had a smile on my face, too.

I'd just saved another life.

All in a day's work for Bernie B.

Chapter 8

MY FRIEND BEAST

A short while later, I stepped into the Dining Hall. I saw Sherman Oaks standing at the first table. He was showing off his watch to a group of third graders.

He was shouting over the roar of loud voices and the clatter of plates and silverware. "This is Function 32," he said. "It's a first-aid kit. Function 33—a powerful halogen flashlight." He beamed the blinding bright light into a kid's face. The poor kid fell off his chair.

"Ooh." "Ahh."

Sherman laughed. "Function 34. It's a portable shower."

The third graders were ignoring their food and gaping in total awe at the watch.

My watch. I knew Sherman would soon be handing it over to me. I just needed a plan....

The third graders were begging Sherman to shine the light into their eyes, too. But Sherman spoke into the watch: "Later, dudes."

His voice boomed over the table. Function 35—

It was also a loudspeaker.

He walked off with his friend Wes Updood. I watched them go to the Nyce House table against the far wall. Sherman started showing off the forty-two functions to Wes and some of his other Nyce House buddies.

With a sigh, I stepped up to the food line.

I picked up a tray and some silverware. Then I saw a crowd of kids down the line. They weren't getting food. They were watching somebody.

Did someone *else* have an awesome watch?

"Hey, what's up?" I pushed through the crowd—and saw my friend Beast at the pizza table.

Yes, that's what everyone calls him. Even his parents call him Beast.

I think it's because...well...he's a *beast*! No one is sure if he's totally human or not. I mean, he walks on all fours some of the time. And he has bristly black hair up and down his arms and his back.

Mrs. Heinie is very tense when Beast is in class. She keeps him on a leash.

I really don't think that's fair. Yes, he growls a lot and chases squirrels on the Great Lawn. And we're not sure what he does after he catches them, but

Beast is a good guy.

The guys in Rotten House all like Beast. He has a bottom bunk in a room on the first floor. But he likes to sleep on the floor.

So, there was Beast at the pizza table. He didn't have a dinner plate or a tray. He picked up an entire pepperoni pizza from the table. Holding it in both hands, he raised it to his face. And shoved the entire pie into his open mouth.

Kids cheered and clapped.

Gulp gulp gulp. Beast swallowed the pie whole. He didn't even chew it!

Kids cheered and clapped some more. A fifth grader slapped him on the back, and Beast let out a disgusting, loud burp that blew back the kid's hair and turned his shirt brown.

Beast swung back to the pizza table. Only one pie left. A huge pizza loaded down with sausages and peppers.

Beast raised the pizza over his head. Then he folded it in half, lowered the whole pie into his open mouth, and swallowed. It made a gross, wet squishing sound as it went down his throat.

Beast smiled. He rubbed his bulging stomach. Then he let out another roaring burp that peeled some of the paint off the wall.

"Ooh, gross," a girl said, making a face. "It isn't funny. It's disgusting."

Yes. Maybe she was right.

But I didn't care. I had a big grin on my face.

Because I knew.

I suddenly knew how I was going to take that watch from Sherman.

Chapter 9

PIE FIGHT

After dinner, I found my pals Feenman and Crench at the Student Center. They were sprawled on couches in the lounge. They were tossing pencils up to the ceiling, trying to make them stick.

This is a difficult sport. You have to get the pencil point to go deep into the ceiling tile. Feenman and Crench practiced pencil-tossing all the time. They had already stuck around twenty pencils up there. Not bad.

"Where's Sherman Oaks?" I asked. "Have you seen him?"

Crench pointed. "He's in the video room with a bunch of kids," he said. "He's showing the new *Spider-Man* movie on his watch."

"Hope he enjoys it," I said. "Because in a few days, all the new movies will be on *my* wrist."

A pencil dropped from the ceiling and stuck into the top of Feenman's head. He didn't even notice. "How, Bernie?" he asked. "How are you going to get the watch?"

"I'm going to challenge him to a pie-eating contest," I said. "No way we can lose. Not with Beast on our side."

Their eyes bulged. "Beast?" Crench said. "You're joking, right? He's an *animal*, Bernie. Know what he did? Beast chased a car down the street this morning."

"And he caught it," Feenman said.

"Trust me," I said. "Trust me."

I ran to the video room. Sherman's movie had just ended. He was popping popcorn on the watch with a special popcorn attachment.

I pulled him aside. "Sherman, what's up, dude?"

"Can't talk now," he said. "I have to make some important phone calls on my watch. Then I'm going to download some new music files."

"I have an idea for a little fun," I said. "A contest between our dorms?"

Sherman's pal from Nyce House, Wes Updood, stepped up to us.

"Whussup, Updood?" I said.

It hurts, but I have to admit it: Wes is definitely the coolest guy in the fourth grade.

He works out. And he knows all the new music. He plays saxophone and blues guitar. And he's the star of Mr. Farrhowt's rap class.

Wes is so cool, he even looks good in a vest!

That's bold.

"Whussup, dude?" Wes Updood said.

"Bernie wants to have a contest," Sherman told him. "Between Nyce House and Rotten Stinking House."

Wes laughed at Sherman's pitiful insult. "Yo, what's up with *that*? What kind of contest, dude?"

"Well…" I rubbed my chin. "How about a pie-eating contest? That would be fun for everyone, wouldn't it? We all like to watch guys stuffing their face with pies, don't we?"

They stared at me. "He's way crazy," Wes told Sherman.

"No. Give it a chance," I said. "We'll make it totally fair. Sherman, you pick a guy from *my* dorm to compete for Rotten House. And I'll pick a guy from Nyce House."

I slapped Wes on the back. "How about Wes here? Wes is a definite winner. You like pie, don't you?"

"Yo, I like *winning*," Wes said, flashing a double thumbs-up.

"Okay, so Wes will go for Nyce House. That means you'll probably win. I don't stand a big chance. But, okay. You pick a guy from my dorm," I said. "Any guy at all. And we'll…uh…have prizes. You know. Just for fun. A nice prize for the winner."

"What kind of prize?" Sherman asked.

"Well…"

I tried to look as if I was thinking hard. "How about if my dorm wins…I get your watch?"

"I KNEW it!" Sherman screamed. "I knew it. It's a cheap trick to take away my watch. No way! No way, Bernie! No contest!"

"But, Sherman, old pal—" I started.

"I'm not falling for it," Sherman cried. "No pie contest. Beat it, Bernie. Beat it!"

Wes stepped up to me and waved a fist in my face. "Dude, I think Sherman wants you to beat it."

"Okay, okay." I turned around and walked to the door.

April-May June stood in the doorway. "Hi," I said. "Have you been thinking about those dance lessons Saturday night?"

"Sherman wants you to beat it," she said.

"Is that a yes?" I asked.

She pointed to the door.

I stepped through the doorway and headed back to Rotten House.

You might think I was defeated. You might think I was a loser tonight. You might think I didn't have a plan to get that pie fight going.

If so, you don't know Bernie B.

Chapter 10

ALLERGIC TO PIE

At lunch the next day, I pulled Beast to the Dining Hall. We stopped at the dessert table. I glanced around the crowded room.

The table where the Nyce House kids always sit was empty. No sign of Sherman Oaks yet.

"Beast, are you ready?" I whispered. I grabbed him by his huge ears to get his attention. "Do you remember what you're supposed to say?"

Beast nodded. "No problem, Big B."

"Okay, buddy. Remember, don't start till Sherman is listening. You sure you remember what to do?"

He grunted. "Ha-ha. We'll put on a little play."

I petted his head. "That's right. A little play."

Was I tense? Yes. Beast and I had rehearsed all morning. But would he remember what to do? Or would he start gobbling blueberry pie?

"Sssh. Here he comes," I whispered. "Here comes Sherman. Get ready, Beast."

He grunted again.

Sherman Oaks picked up a lunch tray and got into the line. I knew he could hear Beast and me. So I started our little play.

I picked a small plate of blueberry pie off the dessert table and handed it to Beast. "Here you go, pal," I said, loud enough for Sherman to hear. "Have some pie."

"Oh, no!" Beast said, shoving the pie back at me. "I can't. Don't make me eat that, Bernie. I'm allergic to blueberry pie."

I acted surprised. "Huh? You're allergic to blueberry pie?"

"Yeah. Allergic," Beast said.

"Come on. Just have a tiny taste," I said.

"No way. If I eat just a tiny taste, I'll get sick and hurl my guts out."

"Too bad, Beast," I said, shaking my head.

"That's really too bad."

I turned and saw Sherman striding over. He had a big grin on his face. "Okay, Bernie," he said. "Maybe I *will* have that pie-eating contest with you. I'll pick Beast to be on your side. Beast against Wes Updood. And it *has* to be blueberry pie."

"But—but—" I sputtered, clapping my hands to my cheeks.

Sherman rubbed his chin. "If I win...let me see...
I need a slave. That's it. If I win, you'll be my slave for
a month. If you win, you can have my watch."

"No way!" I said. "That's not fair. You heard Beast
say he's allergic to blueberry pie. Let me pick another
guy, Sherman. Give me a break. Let me pick someone else for the contest."

Sherman shook his head. He had the biggest grin on
his face. "No. It has to be Beast," he said. "Only Beast.
Beast against Wes Updood. And *all* blueberry pies."

"But I'll lose. I'll lose big-time," I said, shaking
my head. "How about cherry pie? Maybe banana
cream pie?"

"All blueberry pies," Sherman said. "Shake on
it." He stuck out his hand.

I started to shake his hand, then pulled it back.
Started to shake, then pulled back. Finally, I shook
his hand. "You've got a sure thing going," I told
Sherman. "You can't lose."

Sherman tossed back his blond head and
laughed. "Know what I like my slaves to do, Bernie?"
he said. "I like them to carry me on their backs to
Mrs. Heinie's class."

"B-but that's on the *fifth* floor!" I stammered. "I have a bad back, Sherman. All those stairs—"

"Better start working out," Sherman said. He spun away and walked off, laughing his head off.

When Sherman was out of sight, I turned back to Beast. "Good work," I said. "The trap is set. Hey— where's that pie?"

The whole pie was gone from the tray.

Beast rubbed his stomach. He had blueberry stains all over his face.

"Good work," I said again. "This contest is a cinch. The watch is mine! Now I just have one little problem. . . . How do I come up with the pies?"

Chapter 11

25 CHOCOLATE CAKES

Our classroom building looks like an old-fashioned school house. I guess that's how it got its name—the School House.

It's an old, red brick building with a white door in front and long vines of poison ivy clinging to the walls.

Some kids call it Mouse

House. Yeah, you guessed why. The mice outnumber the students two to one. You can't fall asleep in class. The mice will crawl up your legs.

The next afternoon, I was walking out of the School House when I saw April-May by the front door. "Hey, hi!" I called. "How's it going?"

"Fine," she said. She kicked a mouse out of the way and started up the front stairs.

I chased after her. "Looking good," I said. "I like what you did to your hair."

"You can't see my hair. I'm wearing a cap," she replied.

"How about a walk? Or maybe we could hang out at the Student Center?"

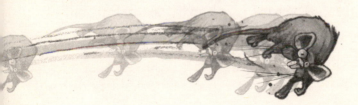

"No way," she said. "I have my cooking class now. With Ms. Monella. It's going to be very cool. We're getting everything ready to bake chocolate cakes tomorrow."

I stepped in front of her. "Chocolate cakes? How many kids are in your class?"

"Twenty-five," April-May said. "We're baking twenty-five chocolate cakes. Get out of my way, Bernie."

My brain was spinning. "Why not blueberry pies?" I said.

She squinted at me. "Are you crazy? It's chocolate cakes." She pushed me out of the way and started into the classroom kitchen.

"About those dance lessons Saturday night—" I said.

She slammed the door in my face.

"Is that a maybe?" I shouted.

I stood there, thinking hard. Chocolate cakes... chocolate cakes...*Why not PIES?*

There's gotta be a way....

Chapter 12

JENNIFER ECCH

I booted a fat mouse from my path and stepped outside. It was a cool, gray afternoon. But my brain was steaming hot. I was picturing twenty-five cakes turning into pies.

"Hey, Big B—what's up?"

Feenman and Crench were calling to me. We started walking across the Great Lawn toward Rotten House.

I explained the problem to them. "The pie-eating contest is a lock," I said. "But how do we get the pies? Any ideas?"

"Run," Feenman said.

"Yeah. Run," Crench said.

"Run? Why?" I asked.

Crench pointed across the lawn. His finger trembled. "Here comes Jennifer Ecch!" he cried.

I turned and saw Nightmare Girl running at me full speed, like a tiger ready to pounce.

"Jennifer Ecch!" I shouted. "RUN!" I took off, my sneakers slapping the ground.

Behind me, I saw Jennifer Ecch soaring across the grass, her brown hair flying behind her head.

She's a big, strong girl, about a foot taller than me. I mean, she's a *really* big girl. Her *knees* are as big as my head!

Someone told me that she's here on an Arm

Wrestling scholarship.

I cut around a flower bed and darted into a bunch of bushes. I glanced back.

Jennifer was gaining on me. She had her hands outstretched, ready to grab me.

Sweat poured down my face as I dove through the bushes and dashed through a clump of apple trees. It's *so embarrassing* to be in fourth grade and have a girl who's madly in love with me.

What could be worse?

I was panting now. I picked up speed as I tore through another clump of bushes.

Behind me, I heard Jennifer's loud cry. She leaped and flew through the air. She tackled me from behind.

I went down hard, landing on my elbows and my knees. My glasses went flying.

Jennifer landed hard on top of me. We were both gasping for breath.

It was a struggle. But I finally pulled her off me. I climbed to my feet and brushed myself off.

"Hey, Jen—" I said. "I was *looking* for you!"

Chapter 13

THE HORRIBLE ACCIDENT

"Huh? Looking for me?" Jennifer Ecch pulled herself to her knees. She wiped grass stains off her hands. She squinted at me with her one blue eye, one brown eye.

"Yeah. I was looking all over for you," I said. I pulled a clump of leaves from my hair. I picked up my glasses.

"Is that why you ran so fast?" she asked.

She stood up and straightened her denim skirt. She had grass stains on those giant knees.

I flashed her my famous, five-star, fifty-two-tooth, dimpled grin.

Jennifer swooned. She gave me a dreamy look.

The dimples get them every time. Sometimes I push a pencil eraser into my dimples to make them deeper.

"Why were you looking for me, Sweet Cakes?" Jennifer asked.

I started to gag. "Please—*please* don't ever call me Sweet Cakes," I begged. "It makes my ears sweat. Really. Look how they're sweating."

"Well, why were you looking for me, Bernie?"

I reached into my pocket for an order form. "Would you like to buy a Bernie Bridges T-shirt? They're made out of rope. But they're very comfortable."

Jennifer let out a roar. She lowered her head, rushed forward, and rammed her head into my stomach.

Ohh. I couldn't breathe! I felt like I'd been hit by a garbage truck. Moaning and groaning, I dropped to the ground. I sprawled on my back, struggling to breathe.

And Jennifer Ecch sat on my chest.

"Is that a no?" I asked.

"I bought *two* of them," she said. "They scratched my skin until I bled. Three days after I stopped wearing them, I was *still* itching like crazy."

I groaned some more. "Get off me, Jen. You're breaking my ribs. I need my ribs. They keep my chest on."

Jennifer didn't budge. "I'll make you a deal, Bernie."

"A deal?"

"I'll get up—if you take dance lessons with me at the Student Center Saturday night."

I choked. "D-d-d-dance lessons? With y-*you?*"

"Bernie, why are you stuttering?"

"Because I think it's a great idea," I said. "D-dance lessons with you. Awesome."

Jennifer let out a squeal. She jumped to her feet. "Really? You want to do it?"

Holding my aching stomach, I stood up slowly. "Yeah. Only I can't do it, Jen. I can't dance. I may never dance again."

I lowered my head sadly. I forced some tears to drip from my eyes.

Jennifer Ecch gazed at me. "Why, Bernie?" she cried. "What's wrong, Sweet Cakes?"

"My knees," I said.

I started to stagger and stumble around, pressing

my knees together. "See? See how I'm walking? Isn't this terrible? I hurt my knees…in a horrible skiing accident."

She squinted at me. "You ski?"

"Well…yeah. And I was caught in an avalanche. A huge snowdrift fell on my knees. Two tons of solid ice. My knees are still frozen stiff! I haven't been able to dance ever since."

I staggered around some more.

"Oh, Honey Bunch, that's so sad!" Jennifer cried. She tried to wrap me in a hug, but I ducked away.

She glanced at her watch. "Oh, no. I'm late for Cooking class. We're getting ready to make cakes."

"I know, I know," I said. "Hey, Jen—do you know any way I could get Ms. Monella to bake pies instead?"

She squinted at me. "Bake pies?"
I nodded.

"If I tell you how, Bernie, will you take the dance lessons with me?"

"Sure," I said. "Dance lessons. No problem." I didn't really hear myself. I was thinking about blueberry pies.

Jennifer smiled at me. "Just ask her. That's all."

"That's your big idea?" I cried. "Just ask her? No way. She'll know it's for one of my schemes. She's much too smart to do anything I ask."

"Not true," Jennifer said. "Sally Monella is a pushover. She's totally soft-hearted. Last week, a kid started crying his eyes out because he missed his mother's hamburgers. So guess what? We all made hamburgers."

My brain started hissing and steaming again. "Crying, huh? Crying worked on her?"

"Yes. Crying always works with Ms. Monella. Gotta run, Sweet Cakes." Jennifer took me by surprise. She grabbed my head and planted a big kiss on my forehead.

Ecch. I took off, running to the dorm to wash it off.

Chapter 14

25 BLUEBERRY PIES

"Okay, Chipmunk—here she comes," I whispered.

We were huddled outside the classroom kitchen. Chipmunk sat on the floor with his head in his lap. I saw Ms. Monella coming down the hall.

"Okay, start crying," I said. "Make it look good, Chipmunk. Don't forget to sob real loud. And move your shoulders up and down."

Chipmunk started to whimper.

"No. No good!" I said, shaking him. "No whimpering—crying. *Sobbing*. Hurry. Get going. Make it good, dude!"

Chipmunk started to sob, shaking his shoulders up and down.

Ms. Monella trotted up to us. "Why, good afternoon, Bernie. How are y'all today?" She has a very soft voice and speaks in a sweet Southern drawl.

"I'm fine," I said. "But…" I pointed to Chipmunk, sobbing his heart out.

"Oh, my goodness!" Ms. Monella exclaimed. "What's wrong with your friend?" she asked me.

"It's because of his birthday," I said. "His birthday is

coming up. His mom always bakes him a blueberry pie for his birthday. It's the first year he won't have one."

I nudged Chipmunk in the back, and he let out some really loud sobs. He kept his head down, weeping hard.

Ms. Monella shook her head. "Ah think ah have an idea," she told me.

She turned to my sobbing friend. "Chipmunk, don't cry," she said. "We *were* going to bake chocolate cakes for the School Bake Sale—but forget that. I'll go buy a bushel of blueberries. And I'll have everyone in my class bake a blueberry pie."

She patted his quivering shoulders. "Cheer up, Chipmunk," she said. "We'll bake *twenty-five* blueberry pies tomorrow, and you can come choose one for your birthday!"

I grabbed Chipmunk by the back of the neck and pulled his head up. "Look. He's smiling already!" I said. "You've made him so happy, Ms. Monella."

She smiled, too. "Well, that's just wonderful. I'd better get to the store and buy up all their blueberries."

"Yes. Definitely. Go to the store," I said. A grin

crossed my face. "Yes. Twenty-five pies. That should be about right."

I felt my wrist. It started to tingle.

Whoa! Of course my wrist was tingling. Tomorrow night I'd be wearing the watch on that wrist!

Chapter 15

EAT PIE!

The next night, we waited till midnight. Then we snuck out of the dorm.

Belzer, Feenman and Crench, Chipmunk, Beast, and a bunch of other Rotten House guys followed me to the School House.

It was a cold, windy night. No moon or stars in the sky. I knew I wasn't shaking from the cold. I was shaking with excitement. And my wrist was tingling stronger than ever.

We trotted across the Great Lawn. When we passed the statue of I. B. Rotten, I touched his bright red nose for good luck.

Sherman and Wes Updood and a gang of other kids were waiting for us at the School House door.

Belzer opened the door for us, and we crept inside. The building was dark except for a few dim ceiling bulbs.

No one said a word as we climbed the stairs to the classroom kitchen. The only sounds were the scampering of mice over the floor and the thud of our shoes on the concrete steps.

I could smell the blueberry pies from the hallway. Yessss!

We pulled open the doors. Clicked on the overhead lights. *And there they were!*

The pies were lined up on a long table against the wall. They were covered in aluminum foil. The room smelled so sweet. I stood in the middle of the room, sniffing with my eyes shut, a big smile on my face.

I felt a tap on my shoulder. Sherman Oaks stood next to me. "Bernie, stop sniffing," he said. "We have to start the contest. How's your back? Are you ready to start carrying me to class?"

Wes and Beast pulled up a table. Belzer started to pile blueberry pies on top of it.

"Sherman, you know this isn't fair," I said. "You know I don't stand a chance with Beast. Let me pick someone else for the contest."

Sherman shook his head. "No way," he replied. "It's Beast against Wes."

"I'm begging you," I said, putting my hands together. "Let *me* eat pies instead of Beast."

Sherman frowned at me. "Forget it, slave. It's Wes against Beast." He waved the watch in my face. "If you're a good slave, Bernie, maybe I'll let you touch the watch for a few seconds."

Then he walked off, laughing.

I chased after him. "Sherman, let's call the contest off," I said. "Come on, dude. Be fair."

He shook his head again. "Bernie, it was *your* idea, remember? Stop stalling. Let's see some pie eating."

Okay. You heard me. I gave Sherman every chance, didn't I?

I was playing fair. I gave him a chance to back out. But now, the watch was mine, all MINE!

I walked over to Beast. He sat behind the table, hunched over the largest blueberry pie. He looked a little weird—even for Beast! He was breathing hard, his eyes bulging. Drool was running down his chin.

"Take it slow at first," I whispered. "Don't eat

twenty pies in one gulp. Let Wes Updood think he has a chance."

I turned to the crowd. "Okay, listen everyone!" I shouted. "Let's start the contest. One...two... three...

EAT PIE!"

Chapter 16

THE BIG BARF-OFF

Wes Updood raised the first pie to his mouth. Sherman and his Nyce House pals cheered him on. "Go, Wes! Go, Wes! You go, Wes! Eat pie! Eat pie! You're the Nyce guy!"

Wes opened his mouth wide and took a big bite.

He made a loud noise as he swallowed. Then he pushed the pie to his face and chomped down hard on his second bite.

What's up with Beast? I wondered.

Beast stared at the pile of pies. He didn't pick one up. He just stared.

"Beast! Beast! Yo, Beast!" all of my Rotten House buddies cheered.

But Beast ignored the cheers. He just sat there, gazing at the stack of pies.

Wes made disgusting swallowing sounds as he finished his first pie.

The Nyce House crowd was going wild.

Wes grabbed the second pie on his pile. He jammed it into his face.

He was *two pies* ahead of Beast! He was reaching for his third pie—*and Beast just sat there!*

"Time out!" I shouted. "Time out!" My heart was doing flip-flops in my chest.

I ran up to the table. I shook Beast by the shoulders. "Wake up! Wake up!" I cried. "The contest started! What are you doing? Start eating!"

Beast grunted. "I…I have a problem, Bernie."

"A problem?" I said. "What kind of problem?"

"I'm not hungry," Beast said.

"That's no problem," I said. "Don't stuff yourself. Just eat fifteen pies. That should be enough to win."

"You don't get me," he said. "I'm not hungry. Sherman bet me I couldn't eat fifty cheeseburgers at

dinner. I won the bet. I ate fifty-four cheeseburgers. Now I'm feeling kinda stuffed."

"*Sherman* bet you?" I cried. "Where is he? I'll kill him! He's a cheater! A total cheater!"

Beast let out a huge burp that sent my glasses flying off my face. He had terrible cheeseburger breath.

I felt a tap on my shoulder. Sherman stood beside me. "Is there a problem?" he asked.

"Uh…yes," I said. "These pies are not the right size. They have an eight-inch diameter. *The Pie-Eating Rule Book* says that all pies must have a *twelve*-inch diameter. We'll have to hold the contest some other time."

Sherman shook his head. "Bernie, you want out because you know you don't stand a chance."

Beast rubbed his bulging stomach. "I have a stomachache," he moaned.

I couldn't believe it. All that scheming. All that planning and thinking. And now I was going to lose.

From now on, the only time I'd ever see Sherman's watch was when I carried him to class in the morning.

But I had no choice. No way I could back out now.

I was defeated. Doomed.

"Okay." I sighed. "Let's keep going."

Suddenly, an idea flashed into my mind. "Beast, start eating, dude," I whispered. "If you eat twenty pies, I'll buy you a Snickers bar for dessert."

Beast raised his head. Snickers bars are his favorite. "Can I have two?" he asked.

"Two," I said. "Just eat. Eat, eat, eat."

The contest started again.

Beast grabbed up three pies at once and shoved them into his face. They disappeared in seconds. His face was covered in purple. Blueberries dripped from his hair and down his shirt.

He grabbed two more pies and shoved them into his open mouth.

Grunting, smacking his lips, Beast finished the first stack of pies. Belzer ran over, carrying another stack.

Beast opened his mouth in a powerful blueberry burp that knocked two kids over and peeled some of the wallpaper off the wall. Then he dug into the second stack, slurping and grunting as he ate.

Blueberries poured down his shirt, his pants, into his shoes. His whole face was stained purple. The juice puddled around the table. He shoved pie after pie into his mouth—and didn't bother to swallow!

"Oh, no. Oh, no." Sherman was slapping himself on the head. "Oh, no. Oh, no. He did it to me again. Bernie did it to me again!"

Sherman slapped himself again and again.

Sherman knew he was a loser. He knew the watch was mine.

Score one more victory for the good guys and Bernie B!

Wes Updood kept trying. He picked up his third pie. He started to shove it into his mouth. But he suddenly stopped.

The pie fell from his hand. He stood up. His face was bright purple. His eyes bulged.

"Ohhhh." He let out a groan. He grabbed his stomach with both hands. He opened his mouth—and barfed blueberry gunk all over the table.

Wes heaved again and again, sending up waves of blueberry pie.

Some of the Nyce House kids were standing too close. Wes spewed a gusher of blueberry barf all over them.

Kids ducked and ran for cover.

The Rotten House guys kept on cheering, "Beast! Beast! Beast!" Because he wouldn't stop.

Beast just kept shoving pies down his throat. He didn't stop until all twenty-five pies were gone.

Sherman slapped himself in the head a few more times. "Bernie did it to me again. He did it to me again!" he kept repeating.

With a long, sad sigh, he slid the watch off his wrist and handed it to me. Then he bowed his head and slunk away.

Mine! Mine!

I held the watch up. I let my friends touch it.

Wes Updood was bent over double. He was groaning and moaning. He was covered from head to foot in blueberry barf.

Two of his friends started to carry him from the room.

"Beast! Beast! Beast!" the cheers continued.

Beast stood up to take a bow—and fell facedown into the pile of blueberry barf on the floor. He didn't move.

I slid the watch onto my wrist. It fit perfectly. I liked the feel of gold against my skin.

"Good work, dudes—" I started. But I stopped when I heard footsteps.

Footsteps?

Yes. Echoing out in the hall.

Rapid footsteps, moving closer.

We all froze as the door swung open.

"Ms. Monella!" I cried. "What are *you* doing here?"

Chapter 17

BUSTED

Ms. Monella let out a cry.

April-May June stepped in behind her. She gasped and clapped her hands to the sides of her face.

"Well, goodness gracious. This sure 'nuff looks like some kind of crazy party. What are y'all *doing* in here?" Ms. Monella demanded.

Her eyes wide, she gaped at Beast, facedown in the thick, purple pile of pie. She saw Wes heaving up some more blueberry barf onto the floor.

"Gross! What a disgusting mess!" April-May cried.

"Where are all the wonderful pies?" Ms. Monella

asked. "What have you done with the lovely blue-berry pies?"

I gave her my cutest, most dimply smile. "Well…we had a little contest," I said. "You know. A little birthday party to cheer up Chipmunk."

"But where are all the pies?" Ms. Monella asked again. She raised a hand to her forehead. I guess she was feeling dizzy. "The pies, Bernie? Where are the pies?"

"Well…"

"Remember I told you those pies were for the school Bake Sale?" Ms. Monella said.

"We were going to sell the pies and give all the money to the homeless kids," April-May said.

Gulp.
Gulp. Gulp.

I swallowed hard. "The homeless kids?"

Ms. Monella's face turned angry. "Who is respon-sible for this?" she asked. "Ah'm afraid he'll have

to come with me to the Headmaster's office."

"It was all Bernie's idea," Sherman said. "I tried to talk him out of it. I told him he was breaking all the rules. I begged him. But Bernie wouldn't listen to me."

Uh-oh. A bad moment for Bernie.

Think fast, Big B. *Think fast.*

"Wait," I said. "I have something for the homeless kids. This is *better* than a bake sale."

I pulled off the watch and held it up. "This watch is worth five hundred dollars. I'm donating it to the homeless kids."

My hand shook as I

handed it to Ms. Monella. I watched the gold disappear as she wrapped her hand around it.

Gone…gone forever.

"Why, thank you, Bernie," she said. "That's so wonderful and generous of you. Now start cleaning up this classroom before I pound your butt."

DANCE LESSONS

We found mops and buckets in the supply closet and started to wash up the piles and puddles of blueberry gunk. Dazed, I swished the mop back and forth. But I didn't see the floor. All I saw was that watch.

I had it in my hands...*in my hands*—for less than a minute. Tragic. Tragic.

I felt a tap on my shoulder. I turned to see Belzer behind me. He had a worried look on his face.

"Bernie, you're standing in the bucket," he said.

I glanced down and saw my shoe in the bucket.

My pants leg was covered in purple goo. I felt too bad to move it.

Feenman and Crench came over. Feenman slapped me on the back. "Cheer up, Big B," he said, grinning. "We won the pie-eating contest!"

"Yeah. We beat those Nyce House bums!" Crench said.

I looked at my three buddies one by one. Did any guy ever have better friends in the world?

"You're right!" I said, stepping out of the bucket. "We won! We won the contest! Rotten House RULES! Nyce House lost—big-time!"

We all cheered and pumped our fists in the air and slapped one another a lot of high-fives and did the secret Rotten House handshake.

"Shut up and mop," Ms. Monella said.

The next night, I wandered to the Student Center, thinking hard. I needed a plan, a new scheme to take my mind off that watch.

I was thinking so hard, I didn't even see April-May come up to me. She grabbed me by the shoulders and shook me to get my attention.

She smiled at me. "Bernie, when you gave that watch away last night, that was the most *generous* thing I ever saw in my whole life," she said. "Maybe you're *not* a totally scheming, selfish, egomaniac creep, after all!"

A compliment!

Do you believe it? A *compliment* from April-May!

"The dance lessons are just starting," April-May said. She took my hand and started to pull me down the hall. "Come on. Let's take them together."

Yesssss!

Victory! Victory!

Who needs a stupid watch? Bernie *is* *king* again!

We walked about four steps when I heard a shout behind me. Then I heard the thunder of running footsteps.

I cried out as strong arms wrapped around me and someone tackled me hard from behind.

"Ooof!" I fell flat on the floor on my stomach. I whipped around—and stared up at Jennifer Ecch.

"There you are, Sweet Cakes!" she gushed. "Time for our dance lessons. You promised, remember? Let's go."

She swung me over her shoulder and carried me down the hall, screaming, "You're MINE! All MINE!"

April-May stood frozen in the hall with her mouth hanging open. "Bernie—?" she called.

Bouncing on Jennifer Ecch's big shoulder, I sadly watched April-May fade into the distance. "April-May!" I shouted. "I have one question I have to ask you!"

"A question? What is it?" she shouted back.

"Would you like to buy a T-shirt?"

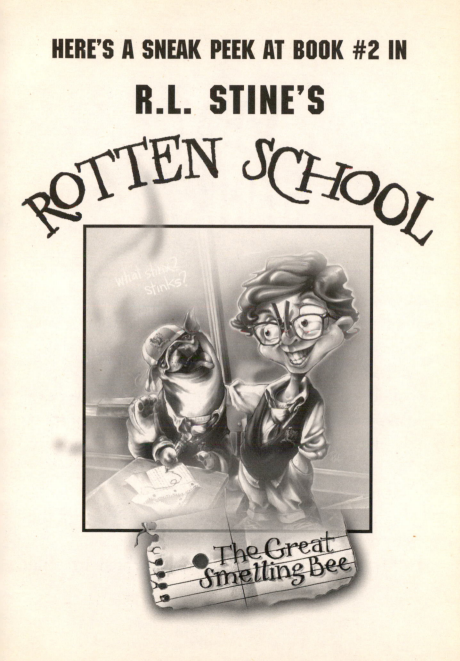

WHAT STINKS?

We heard more scratching sounds, and then a loud *squaaaawk*. Something was definitely alive in there. We had to get that box open—fast!

Belzer found tools in the basement. They went to work, prying open the lid. I did the most important job—I cheered them on. "Let's go, dudes! Good job! Good job!"

It meant a lot to them.

A few minutes later, the lid popped up, and the front of the box fell to the floor with a crash.

My mouth dropped open as I stared in total

disbelief at two animals.

A dog and a parrot.

MY dog and MY parrot!

"My pets!" I cried. I dove forward and dropped to the floor of the crate to hug my fat, sloppy bulldog.

Lippy, my beautiful green parrot, stood in his cage on his perch and squawked, *Go bite a WALNUT!*"

Isn't he sweet? Who taught him to say that? Was it me?

"Go bite a WALNUT!"

Ha-ha. He cracks me up.

I hugged my dog. "Good to see you, fella!"

He snorted hello and drooled drippy stuff all over the front of my school blazer.

Belzer stuck his head into the crate. "But, Bernie, where's the TV?"

"There's no TV. It's my pets from home!" I cried. "I guess they missed me so much, Mom and Dad shipped them to school."

I felt so happy. I'd really missed my pets. And now here they were. Awesome!

I jumped up and smoothed Lippy's feathers. "Are you a good boy, Lippy?" I whispered to the parrot.

"Are you a pretty boy?"

"*Eat birdseed and CHOKE!*" Lippy squawked.

Isn't he *cute?*

Feenman and Crench dropped down on their knees and started to pet my big bulldog. We heard a loud *BRAAAAAT*. The dog let out a moan. They suddenly stopped petting him.

Feenman made a horrified face. "Ooh, what STINKS?" he gasped.

"The dog!" Crench cried. "Bernie—your dog—he STINKS! Oh, it's bad. It's BAD!"

"Hold your breath," I said. "It'll go away in a minute or two."

"I *am* holding my breath!" Belzer cried. "It doesn't help!" The poor guy had tears running down his cheeks. He staggered away, choking, his fingers pressed to his nose.

"Oh, man, that's BAD!" Feenman groaned.

Crench dove for the window, pulled it open, and stuck his head outside.

"Bernie, what's your dog's name?" Feenman asked.

"Gassy," I said.

Feenman nodded. "Good name."

ABOUT THE AUTHOR

photo by Dan Nelken

R.L. Stine graduated from the Rotten School with a solid D+ average, which put him at the top of his class. He says that his favorite activities at school were Scratching Body Parts and Making Armpit Noises.

In sixth grade, R.L. won the school Athletic Award for his performance in the Wedgie Championships. Unfortunately, after the tournament, his underpants had to be surgically removed.

R.L. was very popular in school. He could tell this because kids always clapped and cheered whenever he left the room. One of his teachers remembers him fondly: "R.L. was a hard worker. He was so proud of himself when he learned to wave bye-bye with both hands."

After graduation, R.L. became well known for writing scary book series such as The Nightmare Room, Fear Street, Goosebumps, and Mostly Ghostly, and a short story collection called *Beware!*

Today, R.L. lives in a cage in New York City, where he is busy writing stories about his school days. Says he: "I wish everyone could be a Rotten Student."

for more information
about R.L. Stine,
go to www.rottenschool.com
and www.rlstine.com